Topic: Spring Animals and Plants   **Subtopic:** Seeds / Garden

Notes to Parents and Teachers:

The books your child reads at this level will have more of a storyline with details to discuss. Have children practice reading more fluently at this level. Take turns reading pages with your child so you can model what fluent reading sounds like.

REMEMBER: PRAISE IS A GREAT MOTIVATOR!

Here are some praise points for beginning readers:

- I love how you read that sentence so it sounded just like you were talking.
- Great job reading that sentence like a question!
- WOW! You read that page with such good expression!

Book Ends for the Reader!

Here are some reminders before reading the text:

- Use your eyes to follow the words in the story instead of pointing to each word.

- Read smoothly and with expression. Read like you are talking. Reread sections of the book to practice reading fluently.

- Look for interesting illustrations and words in the story.

Words to Know Before You Read

bee

flowers

honey

hose

pollen

seeds

shovel

watering can

Planting
SEEDS

By Carolyn Kisloski

Illustrated by
Isabella Grott

Rourke
Educational Media
rourkeeducationalmedia.com

It is spring. Mom and I are planting seeds.

"Can you go get the seeds?"
asked Mom.

"Mom, come look at this bee.
It likes the flowers," I said.

"When the seeds grow, many bees will come," said Mom.

"Bees get pollen from flowers. Then they can make honey," said Mom.

"Wow, the bees are good for us. Thank you, bees!" I said.

"Which seeds will we plant?"
I asked.

"All of them. You can choose," said Mom.

"Let's plant daisies first," I said.

"Okay. We need the shovel and water," said Mom.

13

"First, we dig a hole. Next, put the seed in the hole."

"Last, water the seed. We will do this for every seed," said Mom.

I fill the watering can with water. "It is too heavy to carry," I said.

"Dad will be home soon. You can ask him for help," said Mom.

"There's a hole in the watering can! I am getting wet!" I shouted.

"We can use the hose instead," said Mom.

"Do you need some help?" asked Dad.
"Dad, you came just in time!" I said.

"Let's plant the seeds together," said Dad.

21

Book Ends for the Reader

I know...

1. Why do bees come when the seeds grow?

2. What do they need to plant daises?

3. What was wrong with the watering can?

I think ...

1. Have you ever planted seeds?

2. When was it and what did you plant?

3. Did the seeds grow?

Book Ends for the Reader

What happened in this book?

Look at each picture and talk about what happened in the story.

About the Author

Carolyn Kisloski has been a life-long teacher, currently teaching kindergarten at Apalachin Elementary School, in Apalachin, NY. She is married and has three grown children. She enjoys spending time at the beach and the lake, playing games, and being with her family. Carolyn currently lives in Endicott, NY.

About the Illustrator

Isabella was born in 1985 in Rovereto, a small town in northern Italy. As a child she loved to draw, as well as play outside with Perla, her beautiful German Shepherd. She studied at Nemo Academy of Digital Arts in the city of Florence, where she currently lives with her cat, Miss Marple. Isabella also has other strong passions: travelling, watching movies and reading - a lot!

Library of Congress PCN Data

Planting Seeds / Carolyn Kisloski

ISBN 978-1-68342-737-7 (hard cover)(alk. paper)
ISBN 978-1-68342-789-6 (soft cover)
ISBN 978-1-68342-841-1 (e-Book)
Library of Congress Control Number: 2017935452

Rourke Educational Media
Printed in the United States of America, North Mankato, Minnesota

© 2018 Rourke Educational Media

www.rourkeeducationalmedia.com

Edited by: Debra Ankiel
Art direction and layout by: Rhea Magaro-Wallace
Cover and interior Illustrations by: Isabella Grott